Kay Winters

# Who's Coming for Christmas?

illustrated by

Jeannie Winston

hearing church bells ring?

Who's that . . .